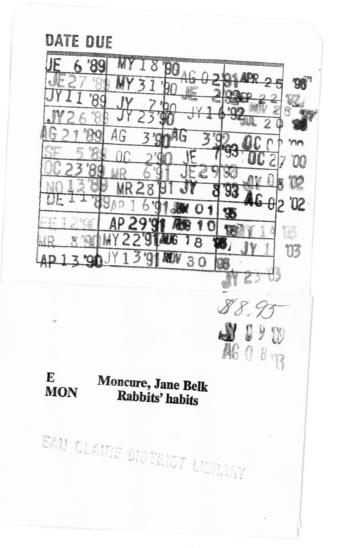

DATE DUE

JE 6 '89	MY 18 '90	AG 02 '91	APR 25 '96
JE 27 '89	MY 31 '90	JE 2 '92	AP 22 '97
JY 11 '89	JY 7 '90	JY 16 '92	NV 26 '97
JY 26 '89	JY 23 '90	AG 3 '92	JUL 20
AG 21 '89	AG 3 '90	AG 3 '92	OC 00
SE 5 '89	OC 2 '90	JE 7 '93	OC 27 '00
OC 23 '89	MR 6 '91	JE 29 '93	JY 03 '02
NO 13 '89	MR 28 '91	JY 8 '93	AG 02 '02
DE 11 '89	AP 16 '91	JW 01 '95	
FE 12 '90	AP 29 '91	AG 10 '95	MY 14 '03
MR 8 '90	MY 22 '91	AUG 18 '95	JY 1 '03
AP 13 '90	JY 13 '91	NOV 30 '95	
		JY 23 '03	

$8.95

JY 09 '09
AG 08 '13

E   Moncure, Jane Belk
MON   Rabbits' habits

Rabbits' Habits

Do you know . . .

A library is a magic castle with many Word Windows in it?

What is a Word Window?

If you answered, "A book," you're right.

A book is a Word Window because the words, and the pictures that tell about the words, let you look and see many things. Books are your windows to the wide, wide world around you.

CHILDRENS PRESS
HARDCOVER EDITION
ISBN 0-516-05722-7

CHILDRENS PRESS
PAPERBACK EDITION
ISBN 0-516-45722-5

© 1988 The Child's World, Inc.
Elgin, IL
All rights reserved. Printed in U.S.A.

Library of Congress Cataloging in Publication Data

Moncure, Jane Belk.
   Rabbits' habits.

   (Magic castle readers)
   Summary: Three little rabbits exhibit both good and bad habits regarding their attitudes toward new experiences, taking care of their things, behaving with others, getting enough rest, and eating healthy foods.
   [1. Rabbits—Fiction.   2. Behavior—Fiction]
I. Peltier, Pam, ill.   II. Title.   III. Series: Moncure, Jane Belk.   Magic castle readers.
PZ7.M739Rad   1988   [E]   87-12841
ISBN 0-89565-406-7

Rabbits' Habits

by Jane Belk Moncure
illustrated by Pam Peltier

Created by

Distributed by CHILDRENS PRESS®
Chicago, Illinois

The Library —
A Magic Castle

Come to the magic castle
When you are growing tall.
Rows upon rows of Word Windows
Line every single wall.
They reach up high,
As high as the sky,
And you want to open them all.
For every time you open one,
A new adventure has begun.

Susie opened
a Word Window.
Here is what she read.

Once there were three little rabbits.

The first little rabbit had a habit of dropping his things here and there.

The second little rabbit had a habit
of leaving his things everywhere.

The third little rabbit had a habit of
putting his things where they belonged.

Which rabbit had a good habit?

One day the three little rabbits hopped to the park to play.

One little rabbit had a habit of pushing and punching to get his way.

One rabbit had a habit of pulling and pinching so he could be first in line.

But one little rabbit had a habit
of waiting his turn.

Which rabbit had a good habit?

13

On Saturday, Papa Rabbit said, "Let's plant a garden."

He gave each little rabbit some garden tools.

The first rabbit sat in the wheelbarrow and said, "I will not."

He had a habit of saying this.

The second rabbit started to dig.
But he soon stopped.

"I cannot," he said. He had a habit
of saying this.

The third little rabbit said, "Come on. Let's go." He went right to work . . .

and finished the job. Which rabbit had a good habit?

When Monday came, it was time to get up and go to school. One rabbit had . . .

a habit of "Early to bed; early to rise." He was ready when the school bus came.

One rabbit had a habit of staying up
very late at night and sleeping . . .

very late in the morning, so he missed
the school bus.

One rabbit got up early. But he had a
habit of playing instead of getting ready.
So he missed the school bus too.

Which little rabbit had a good habit?

On Tuesday, in gym class, the rabbits had a race.

One rabbit cried because he did not win. He had a habit of crying.

One rabbit frowned because he did not win.

He had a habit of frowning.

One little rabbit smiled even though

he did not win. "I will try again," he
said. "Maybe I will win next time."

Which rabbit had a good habit?

On Wednesday, all three little rabbits
hopped to the school picnic. Do you
know why they were all smiling?

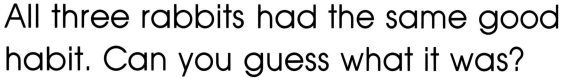

All three rabbits had the same good
habit. Can you guess what it was?

The rabbits ate good food. They ate lots of fresh fruit, lots of vegetables,

and grains such as wheat, oats, corn, and rice.

What a nice rabbit habit!

You can have good habits too.
You can be like these rabbits.

A happy rabbit.

A sharing rabbit.

A helpful rabbit.

A caring rabbit.

A loving rabbit.

A friendly rabbit.

A nice rabbit.

A healthy rabbit.

Hop! Hop!